Illusions, Delusions
By
Alexander Raphael

A collection of short stories

Cover artwork and profile photo by Meg Sorick

Order of Stories

1. Within Twilight

2. After Life

3. Breaking Through the Fourth Page

4. Punbelievable

5. Just Imagining, Today

6. Death = New Life

7. Questions, Answers, Questions

Background Notes

Within Twilight

It was the most spectacular sight with the most spectacular sounds. The sky was filled with all kinds of kaleidoscopic colours. Red and white and orange and gold and silver and purple and brown and green and blue, with every shade in-between. There were diamonds and emeralds, rubies and sapphires and clouds and planets and comets that moved around at the speed of light in all directions with the sparkling sounds being heard far below.

Fireworks were being generated every second, in the form of famous tourist attractions. The Great Wall of China, the Coliseum, the Grand Canyon, Iguazu Falls. One after the other, which morphed into the Seven Wonders of the World, and then became animals. Elephants became giraffes, then rhinos, then lions, tigers, whales, monkeys and birds. Music by Vivaldi and Mozart and Beethoven and Strauss came straight from the sky, before the figures came to life in the form of velvet stars.

The Magician was putting on quite the show for his enthralled guests. No one said a word as one visual phenomenon followed another. All they could do was stare at amazement as the stranger, dressed immaculately in a silken robe whose designs were changing every second, continued to weave his magic. In a world before major technology, this Magician had come from the gods.

And things were far from finished. The sky above suddenly became a horizontal mirror, reflecting every last detail of the town and people watching. This being, who had appeared from out of nowhere just minutes before, ramped up the illusionary appeal. He zoomed in on the sky as though it were a magnifying glass, showing the closest of details to the people on the ground.

He held up his finger, to show that there was one last trick left. He tapped it into the air at his own rhythm almost as though he was conducting his own orchestra. And then he smiled. With that his fingers and outstretched arm came back to his side. And then the ground started to move. There was a tilt of a slight angle as the crowd began to lift off from where they were standing. But they weren't leaving the ground, rather the ground was coming with them. And the sky was making space by tilting too. Within seconds they had swapped completely. Quite impossibly, those on the ground were now looking down at the sky below.

Rather than rotate back, he decided to let the group be in on the magic. He created five different ways for them to get back down. The first person used a slide, one floated down on feathers, another was transported with two clicks of a finger while the fourth jumped and landed immediately. Most fantastically, a young girl changed into a bird before flying down to the ground and changing back to her previous form.

Without anyone noticing, the sky and ground had reverted to their conventional positions. And the Magician had not moved once.

"What does this mean?" asked the mesmerised young girl, still waving her arms as though they were wings. She was about five, with innocence and wonder still a big part of her soul. She was smiling but still unsure why this was all happening.

"Why does it have to mean anything?" he replied in a soft yet immense voice. "Why does everything have to have meaning? Sometimes beauty is just beauty. And imagination is imagination."

Another spoke out. "Where did you come from?" What do you want?" He was old and suspicious and cynical but still curious and there was space for hope.

"I have powers. More than I know how to deal with. More than you can ever imagine."

"But who are you?", the old man persisted. "And why can we see you but others can't?"

The Magician hesitated, as though he was torn between patience and impatience, honesty and deception. There was an enraptured silence, as all eyes were on this extraordinary figure, whose face was hidden by the robe he was wearing.

He looked down, which some thought was shyness while others felt it was merely part of his bearing.

"You ask many questions. I have already seen so much. If I told you everything, then you would still not know everything. Not all questions need answers and not all questions have answers. I appeared because I had a desire to. And soon I will go home. But before I do, I will leave you with something. Come closer."

The group of five shifted in so they could almost touch him. Some did, which made him push their hands away.

"I don't need you to touch me. I need you to believe me. I will grant you each a wish. You may ask me one request and I will immediately make it be."

There were excited murmurs within the crowd. Suddenly a suspicious voice rang out. "Hold it. How do we know this isn't a trick?"

The Magician shone a light to see the man near the back in further detail. In his early 20s, clean shaven, with wavy auburn hair, glasses and a thin green jacket and dark blue trousers. There was a silence for a few seconds and everyone wondered how the Magician would respond.

He began changing the man's appearance. He made him have red hair, black hair, blond hair, dreadlocks, long hair, bald. Suddenly he had a goatee, a white beard, thick sideburns, a scar, a small facial tattoo. He expanded the man's waistline slightly wider and then slimmer as though he were playing an accordion. A smart suit, army fatigues, a dinner jacket were also experimented with, as were pyjamas, prison jumpsuit and head to toe in denim, leather and then suede.

Replacing the man's original image, he looked at him with a sense of exasperation. "I am offering you an opportunity. I am the Magician and I can make things happen. Live here, live now. Think creatively. Be different. Everything you can imagine is real."

The man, like with the rest of the crowd, nodded in awe and amazement.

The Magician continued, unflustered by the interruption. "I did consider one wish decided by the five of you, but that felt so restrictive. And it would take aeons for you all to decide. And so, one individual wish. There are two caveats. No resolution to all wars, no resolution to hunger and famine, no formulation of love potions or ideas of time travel."

He saw confusion, but no grievances. They could not understand all the words by this majestic being but were fascinated and did not want to go anywhere."

"I'm glad you all acquiesce", said the Magician as a numbered golden light suddenly appeared above each person. "You'll see the light above you. That is the order I would like you to ask in."

The group of five quickly and quietly got into the correct order. Around them, people were walking past all the time but could not see the Magician or the crowd. The Magician made an apple appear and took a bite. The bite disappeared and the apple became whole again. He took several more bites, with the same thing happening each time, before he then threw it into the sky where it landed in a bin that instantly appeared. And then it was all gone in a second. The crowd gasped but said nothing.

"The second is this. There is a risk the wish doesn't go quite to plan. I can't guarantee you will be happy with what you wish for. I can control the images you see, but real, live things are harder, more unpredictable. But yes, there is a good chance of success. No more explanations and no hesitations please. I am only here for a short time and must get back."

A slim, redheaded woman spoke with some assurance. "I'd like £300,000 immediately, please." There were loud gasps from the group. That would make her the richest person in the land.

With that, the money appeared. But rather than in notes, it was in coins. Hundreds of bags, filled with coins. The woman went to pick them up but the bags were too heavy to carry and coins were spilling out. People outside of the group, astonished at seeing coins appear from nowhere, were running from all over to take what they could. The woman who had made the wish was only able to keep a small amount.

Aware that outsiders might stay and get suspicious, he sent them to a remote island. There was no one there to disturb them, the only sound being the waves crashing against the beach, accompanied by coins. To emphasise the point of isolation, he changed the sky and all around to be clouds. Bored, he changed the view all around them to revolving landscape paintings from Cezanne, Van Gogh, Turner, Monet and many more.

Having noticed that the woman with the first wish had few coins, he produced a large bag and gave her one. In that moment, he also filled people's hands with coins.

"Fine. Let that be the end of that desire. Ok, who's next?" The Magician noticed a hand go up by the five-year-old girl from earlier. Her poverty was obvious from her outfit, but she had the sweetest and most genuine of smiles.

She walked up towards the Magician and said: "Thank you for granting me this wish. This is my favourite doll Tina. As long as I have her, I won't need any other presents. I want my doll to be as good as new and that I will never lose her again."

With that she held out her hand and showed her rather tatty doll. The Magician took a long hard look at her, then completely changed her appearance to look like what it had once done. It looked pristine. What once was knotted hair, torn dress and dirty hands and face was now new enough that could go on sale at the finest fair. The girl looked delighted. She held her close and could have sworn it said something back to her. She looked around but it became clear no one else could hear anything. She smiled again.

"It's me next! My turn." A guy of about 20 waved his hands theatrically and pointed to the number above his head to ensure he had the Magician's full attention. "I want to see the princess. If I see her then I can tell her how much I want her. I know exactly what to say to win her over."

There was a slight murmur as they all knew how beautiful the princess was. She lived in a far-off land and they had only seen her when she had made rare state visits.

"As you desire." Like with the first wish, there was a slight puff of smoke. When the smoke cleared, the crowd saw the young man in question swinging on a rope across the ocean. Birds passed him as he swept over the waves. He could not believe the sensation as he looked down on the world beneath him. He could see through the cool, clear water and see and hear the whales and dolphins and every kind of fish. He could almost feel the water on his skin.

And he could see the palace approaching. It was quite something. With wealth beyond civilization, it was even more than he had imagined. Gold everywhere. The most intricate designs and skilled architecture. Guarded by two dozen knighted soldiers. But this rope was going through. Right over them. And they didn't see him.

He flew right through a window and landed in the princess' room. He looked in a mirror and could see his reflection. This was it. The moment he had dreamed of for the past five years. And now it was happening. He landed inside her room. But she was napping. He went to call to her, to wake her up. But as he went to her, he knocked a table leg and though the princess remained asleep, her dog, sleeping quietly in the corner, woke and started growling. With that, the guards from within the building started to go to the room. Before anything happened, he realised he was right back with the Magician and the small group.

"That's not fair, she was asleep! I barely even saw her. She didn't see me or even hear me!"

The Magician looked at him with a slight hint of a smile. "I can't control your dreams or what the people are doing at this very moment. I can only make them happen. The good and bad of how it turns out is outside of my control. I could easily have left you there. That would have been rather amusing actually. Now, who is next?"

A shy woman in her early 40s spoke quietly. "I have never been deemed attractive by the wider population. As such, I've been ignored by people I wanted to notice me. I want to be strikingly beautiful."

The Magician said nothing, and granted the wish. With that, the woman was indeed prettier. But rather than the dowdy dark-haired lady with an ill-fitting hairstyle and poor complexion she was before, she was now an Amazonian style goddess, long-limbed and with an aura that radiated grace, power and independence. The Magician created a mirror for her to look into. It was nothing like the face she had before and would take some time for her to get used to, but she knew she would.

There was a rather long silence as an old man shuffled out onto the front. He breathed heavily and tightly gripped his walking stick. He had paid no attention to those around him or wondering what they thought of him. His eyes had seen a lot of pain.

"I am old and I know death is not far away. I know not who you are or what you want. But you seem to have powers that are greater than anything I have ever seen. And so, I ask you. My wife wrote me a special letter after we celebrated 20 years together. She is gone, and the letter was stolen among expensive, replaceable things a few years ago. I can remember a lot of it but not all. I wish I had that letter back to keep forever."

The Magician's expression didn't change, though for the first time his robe had stopped its illuminations. He momentarily slid his palms up and down together before he produced a four-page letter. There was a great silence as the man collected the letter and his eyes filled with tears. Those listening attentively would have heard a very quiet but heartfelt thank you.

The Magician clapped his hands, but as he looked around, he realised there was one person still to be fulfilled. His illuminations had returned, and though appearing distracted, spoke loudly.

"Come now, you are the last to be granted a wish. What will you ask for?"

The man, in his late twenties, hesitated. He was nervous and began to pace around in all directions. "I'm not sure. I want to be a gifted violinist. I want to live to 100. I want to go to New York. I want to stay in perfect health. I want to never have to work again. I want…"

He looked up and the Magician was gone. As was everybody else.

After Life

Four old men sit quietly among the shadows of a cemetery playing 21.

Atlantis studiously stares at his cards, though he knows they are no good. Knowing that his cards are too low to win, and too high to be worth gambling on another, he decides he would rather stick with his cards. After this, he thinks so loudly no one can hear him, like he has been doing for the last 20 years. He thinks back to a time when life was so different, and he belonged in a world that embraced rather than exiled him. When he was king of the castle, king of the urban jungle, king of the world that he had created for himself. When he was the "golden boy" of the family, the one with the future. That time is gone, a distant dream that seems so much closer the longer time goes on. Atlantis knows he is in a room with a view, a goldfish bowl, a glass house, yet no one is looking in and he is not looking out. He knows his moment of glory is gone, his moment is gone on a journey into a forbidden world that he no longer has the heart, body or soul to fight for. He has been knocked out of the ring, is out of the circle, is standing without a key staring at a locked door. The time when people read his books has gone, the time when he could write those books was bypassed before that. Atlantis knows there is not much left but the inevitable end. Given the choice if he could live again, he would take it, if only to relive those utopian days when his future was something to look towards, not something to look back on.

El Dorado is not sure what to do with his cards. Stroking his long beard, he wonders whether it is worth risking. Though it is a while, the others don't look up. They are used to his slowness. He eventually asks the banker for more cards, though the next one takes him over the limit and he confesses his 'crime'. As he does this, he thinks back to the past like he frequently does, a past that seems like yesterday. Because in a sense, life is only yesterday, today and tomorrow. And he would rather live in yesterday than today, because tomorrow is only going to become today. He can distort yesterdays, but knows that he cannot manipulate tomorrows. His life was never that fascinating, he has not fallen from so great a metaphorical height as Atlantis has, though El Dorado does not know this. He was neither married or engaged, and unlike Atlantis, cannot use misfortune as an excuse, though he does as it is the only way he knows he can survive. His truth is more important, and it is the only truth that continues to exist. Given the choice of living his life again, he is not sure whether he would take it. All his risks have generally been unsuccessful.

Olympus is pleased with his cards. Asking for another card, he gains a Jack taking him to 20. He decides to stick with this, knowing he has a good chance of victory. He stares at his cards studiously, despite knowing the decision was effectively already made for him. Knowing there is still the banker to play, he waits patiently. In effect, he has spent his whole life waiting. Abandoned as a baby, left outside a supermarket without so much as a name, Olympus has always expected an explanation. Time ticks slowly, but he can no longer hear its sound. He knows he is in a place where time means nothing and his once good looks have long faded, and nothing represents whatever is left. Having been surrounded by death for most of his life, he sees things in beginning and end, black and white, dead and alive. Never having taken a risk, and having never been tempted, his life has a regular, if predictable theme. Wondering whether he has enjoyed his life, he knows he has never seen its purpose.

Hades studies their faces before he looks at his cards. He is pleased with them. He knows it would be near impossible to lose. He lays down his cards silently. Life, he reflects, has never really surprised him. It is a series of circumstances in which you have a limited amount of control and there is no point complaining when it rains but to carry on walking. Hades has had a colourful life. Married three times but forgotten by all, outliving his family, ignored by his former friends, Hades knows he had made mistakes. A man of many talents as a teenager, Hades has wasted them all and now has nothing left. He never looks back to his youth because he cannot recognise it. Now a stranger in his own life, merely an extra in his own dream, and an audience to his own stage, he knows there is no possibility of the curtain being raised for a cameo. Asking himself whether he would do things differently given the chance, he knows he may take a different route but would still end up in the same place.

Hades shuffles the cards. Without a word, and without looking up, he deals again.

Breaking Through the Fourth Page

This blank page. It's never a good thing when you have writer's block. The blank page stares back at you, and you know there's a story to be written, countless stories to be written, but the fingers don't seem to be able to work their usual magic. I need some inspiration from somewhere, but the usual places don't seem to be yielding any results.

And I have so many places. The gorgeous view from my window, the artwork on my wall, the books on my shelves, the stories from the newspapers, the inspirational quotes I have everywhere, the notes in my writing books. Right now, they all seem to lead into a cul-de-sac. The hidden worlds of creativity and imagination are blocked by the brick wall of silence and insecurity. I need to try something different.

But what? After all, writing is such an unusual thing. No rules, no restrictions. You get to create something no one could have, and then let them share it. So much has already been written and yet, there will always be so much more to say. And infinite ways of saying it.

I need to try something different. Something different. What would be different?

Start big. Think big. Worry about all the logic later. Or even let someone else worry about it. Why should I be worrying about it? My characters should be doing that. Hang on. That's it! Chat with one of them. After all, they're the ones on set, out living all the adventures and bringing everything to life. They know what works and what doesn't.

And so…

The writer taps his pen. He knows he needs some help.

"Hey Bob."

I don't like the name Bob, it sounds more like a verb. And it's an abbreviation.

"Just the first name that came to mind. What name do you want?"

Something with a bit of razzmatazz. Maybe Raz, maybe Mataz. I want something that makes me stand out from the rest of the characters you have created. How about...

"Hey, hang on a second. I'm the writer. I'll give you a name. Something different, huh? Hmmm. How about ID?"

It better not be short for idiot! How about we change the initials to AD?

"No, no, no. It's ID. You wanted an identity remember. How about... (*Tapping irritatingly for several seconds*) ... got it! Indigo Deep. Makes you original yet somehow linked to Indiana Jones. A cousin or something. And as you're Indigo, you can be a colourful character. Wahey!"

Funny man. Mind you, it does make me sound like I'm going to have all these exciting adventures. And I know you don't write the action suspense stories, but if you want to have me sword fighting on a pirate ship, or in a race against time against a ticking time bomb or in an epic family saga covering a century, I can do that too. I'm very gifted. I have quite the range. I make a very convincing woman too.

"That's good to know. You've never complained whatever setting I've put you in. You always deliver your lines well. And you do work well with others. Actually, where are the others?"

I know how you work. You don't start off thinking of other characters before you have the main character nailed down.

"True. You do know me well."

Yeah, well I'm the one who has to rehearse with them once you've switched your computer off. We don't just sit around waiting for you. We practice the dialogue and the mannerisms. And keep the emotions. Quite a pain when you decide to make big changes.

"So much of writing isn't what you write, but what you don't. You have to leave the reader space for their own interpretations too."

I get that. Just wish you'd work that out sooner sometimes.

"You and me both!"

That's not the worst bit, though. Don't forget the uncredited work I do. You never finished writing that Woody Allen style play.

"A blessing, believe me. It was shocking."

Or the one about the four young boys who go looking for treasure but are never seen again.

"I'd forgotten about that one. Just couldn't get it to work."

Or the one when I want to play in the first team. So, I start killing off all my team mates in unusual ways so as to jump ahead and get my chance. I saw your notes for that. You should definitely write that.

"Kind Hearts and Football Coronets for sure. Real dark comedy potential. I've not completely given up on it."

Excuses, excuses.

"Let's get back on track. I want something brand new. I need to think of what situation to put you in."

I have a few ideas.

"Oh really. Go on."

How about a heroic journey where I have to tackle all these ogres before I meet the beautiful princess? And unlike the really old fairy tales I want it to end with something other than 'happily ever after'. I want to run my own business or go travelling.

"It needs something more original and more modern than that. I'd have to create a big back story or a rival of some kind."

But I couldn't be sure I'd win. I know you. You don't like obvious endings. I've heard you mutter about giving things "an edge". Making things different.

"I could have a set of cameos from all the fairy tale characters. Maybe even video characters too. No, I feel that's been covered recently by modern day animation."

Fine. How about you come up with an idea?

"Arghhhhhhhhhh. Why do you think I brought you to life? You're supposed to be an endless stream of ideas. You have my full attention."

How about my friend really likes this girl and I have to listen to him talk about her all the time and then he finally gets the nerve to ask her, she says no, humiliates him and years later, he decides to get revenge?

"Hey, hey, hey. That was one of my first stories. I'm not taking that cheek. You do realise that unless I write you new material, you're going to be stuck reenacting the same old ones."

Ok, ok. I see your point. Tell you what, why not put some music on. You've done that before.

"Creativity through osmosis. Good idea." (*He tries a few different songs but keeps changing after a few seconds*)

Gah! Just pick one!

(*Keeps skipping songs*) "Wait for it...Not that one. Nope. Not right now. Wrong mood for that. Intro too long. Ok, got it!"

Fine. Let's brainstorm some ideas. How about...?

"You know I saw this band live. Quite an interesting backstory. The best bands tend to have them. So much infighting. One member left just before they made it big. That's got to hurt! Wonder what happens when he hears them on the rad..."

You're getting distracted. And stay away from that TV remote!

"And I haven't even got started. There are tonnes of stories. And I love hearing about the context of songs. Freddie Mercury wrote "Crazy Little Thing Called Love" in the bath. Michael Jackson came up with "Billie Jean" while driving. Deep Purple got "Smoke on the Water" when a fire cancelled their Lake Geneva gig."

That's interesting, but…

"And I like writing my own song lyrics."

You know what? There's probably a story in that.

(*Oblivious*) "You know there's probably a story in that. Hmmmm. I always have to get the title of the short story before I even write the first line. Makes sense to call it after the band. What are the best band names? Nirvana. Joy Division. The Doors. Velvet Underground, Arcade Fire." (*Long gap*)

You've gone quiet.

"Just looking around my room for inspiration. (*Taps pen irritatingly*) Got it! Instinctive. Don't know where that came from, but I like it! Now, I just need to get your character sorted, the rest of the band too. Probably need a band manager in there. Setting, time frame. Ending too. Major events. Things to avoid. What type of music. Already have an idea of how to begin it. Let's try that out."

I'm Indigo Deep remember. Let's do this!

"Yeah, you're not keeping that name."

It's colourful.

"It's cringy."

Worth a try. You and your changes.

"Ready to begin?"

I'm always here. And always ready. Let's go.

Punbelievable

Finley Waters: Man, what a day. Thanks for choosing this restaurant Robin. It was very tweet of you to remember it was my birthday.

Robin Foxton: I saw a blog review that said it ofishially has the best seafood section in town. Would have been shellfish not to share it with you. Especially as we haven't met up since your business trip to Swimapore.

Finley Waters: It shore looks a good plaice. As I was heading out of the office, my colleague looked envious and said "Let minnow what you order."

Robin Foxton: It's been ages since they sat us down. Service cod be a lot better.

Finley Waters: Service bad, food great. That's what I've been herring from everyone. I'll sea if I can get that waiter's attention. Done! Eel be right over.

Waiter: (*Approaches*) Welcome to The Eating Among the Fishes restaurant. I'll be your server today. Sorry for the delay. It sardinely got very busy. Water day! I had to clam a few people down. They were getting a bit crabby. Our reservations system had some problems. Thankfully, it's going swimmingly now.

Robin Foxton: Let's have a bottle of your finest house white. Just for the halibut. And no need to debait this. I'm having the lobster paella.

Finley Waters: I don't need to mullet over either. I'm having the sea bass, fish cakes and tuna salad.

Waiter: Grilliant choices. I'll be right back. (*Leaves*)

Robin Foxton: I swear, that waiter looks like Salmon Rushdie!

Finley Waters: He really does. I wonder if he gets that when he's trout and about. I was just wondering whether to perchase one of his books. Funny old world. Any fin is possible.

Robin Foxton: Ah nice, I've been reading a bit recently. Catfish 22. If you get the opportunaty you just have to read it. I'd add Metamorfifish, Wuthering Pikes and the Jaws of Perception too.

Waiter: (*Approaches*) Here is your bottle. It's dolphinately a fine choice (pours both glasses and then leaves).

Finley Waters: So how are things at work? That new guy sounds useless. Like he was lost at sea and completely out of his depth. And how are things with your new gillfriend? Come on, don't be koi. All I know is that she's a dog lover.

Robin Foxton: Ah yes, Pawline. Mutt have been fate. It's not like I've been active on the dating scene. I've been doggedly after that promotion.

Finley Waters: I know! You've been alsationable on that score. I've not seen you in weeks.

Robin Foxton: Sorry about that. I guess my inner ambition was unleashed after that work trip. Working those long hours has been ruff. I wasn't the only one trying to move up. Would have made a dramatic dogumentary. Real dog eat dog stuff. Being hounded all the time. But since meeting her it doesn't seem to matter. I was probably the underdog anyhow.

Finley Waters: Did you and the mastiff dog lover meet at your vet practice?

Robin Foxton: No, I was on a quick lunch break and literally ran into her at the supermarket. You know me, always dachshund around.

Finley Waters: So, what happened after? Pup and running from the get go?

Robin Foxton: We agreed to go to this fancy Italian restaurant. She was late as she had left her handbag behind and had to go back so she could retriever purse and stuff. Almost made her late for the reservation. I was thinking: "Howl late will she be?"

Finley Waters: People being late. That's my pet hate.

Robin Foxton: It was worth it, though. She looked so fetching. Real elegant restaurant too. The pianist even played Poochini.

Finley Waters: Fur real? That is classy.

Robin Foxton: It turns out we've a really similar sense of humour. She's a big fan of Eddie Lizzard, Tuna Fey, Jelly Seinfeld Anchovy Chase.

Finley Waters: Well, she's got my seal of approval. What does she do?

Robin Foxton: She's a freelance fundraiser for various animal charities and animal shelters. She does so much. And she's so romantic. She's got into the rabbit of baking me animal-shaped cookies. As the weather has been so much otter recently, she's been doing jungle ones.

Waiter: (*Approaches*) Here sir, is your lobster bisque. And also, the sea bass, fish cakes and tuna salad. We've recently added the collieflower to the dish, so any feedback at the end of the meal would be most welcome. (*Leaves*)

Robin Foxton: It's only my second time eating lobster. I won't be wolfing this down! But yeah, things have been going super well. Just remembered. At canine pm, the local store closes and I need to pick up a few things.

Finley Waters: So, pug in the gaps for me. What do you two talk about?

Robin Foxton: She just loves dogs. But she used to have all kinds of pets growing up. Now she has two dogs, Bark Twain and Droolius Caesar. Funnily enough, she also has a cat that shares your birthday.

Finley Waters: You're kitten me?

Robin Foxton: Yeah, pretty ameowsing really. I'm feline good about this. I think it's meant tabby with this one. If anything, I'm worried it's going too purrfectly. But enough about me. I heard there was a bit of a catastrophe on your trip.

Finley Waters: Yeah, we got Kat, our next door neighbour, to keep an eye on the house when we were away and water the plants in the house. You know my wife and I went to a tour of Italy for a break. Real romemantic place.

Robin Foxton: I guess once you're Turin there you forget about life back home.

Finley Waters: Genoally, the best country I've ever visited. You have to go. You're messina out otherwise. Turns out, the neighbour had left the water running. The florence all flooded. Quite a lot ruined. I wanted to give her a pizza my mind. But amid all the comotion you realise it was an honest mistake. She's agreed to cover the repair bill. No point making a fountain out of a molehill.

Robin Foxton: You do live life a lot more Capri spirited than I do. House it going with the recovery?

Finley Waters: You know I believe in karma. If you don't act kindly now, you'll pompeii for it later. Yeah, we got all the new stuff fine.

Robin Foxton: That's wonderful to hear. It will be our six month anniversary tomorrow so I got all this cool stuff booked well in advance, including the biggest bouquet of flowers you've ever seen. Didn't want to leaf it until the last minute.

Finley Waters: Great to see you this happy. You had some tough break ups back in the day. There was Rose, Jasmine, Daisy, Poppy, Violet, Olive, Flora, Iris, Holly, Ivy, Heather and, what was her name again? Oh yeah, Lily. Her mum Hyacinth was always so nice to me. Didn't Lily go abroad after you broke up?

Robin Foxton: That's why we broke up actually. She was an environmentalist. I wanted to sweep her off her feet but that relationship was just littered with mistakes. We've both moved on now though. She's dating a farmer. I always knew someone who worked outdoors would a tractor.

Finley Waters: Awesome. Let's get the bill. Hang on, where's my wallet. This scampi happening. Oh wait, there it is. Freaks me out when I change pockets.

Waiter: (*Approaches and takes plate*) You enjoyed the dishes? I have to ask. The head chef has been grilling me. I said I'd kelp out by finding out what you thought of the new salad? He's been fishing for compliments all day.

Finley Waters: I did. Ah yes, your spacific request. Yeah, all great. Nothing to hake at all. If you can bring over the bill as well, please. (Waiter leaves) Oh, before I forget. Did you know I can jump higher than a house? Because houses can't jump. (Laughs)

Robin Foxton: (*Rolls eyes*) You and your wordplay. You'd never catch me doing that.

Just Imagining, Today

ZZZZZZZZZZZZZ.

Yesterday was a long night, muttered Ashley Mitten to himself as he awoke to a new day and his alarm clock going off. He sure had meant to go to bed earlier.

X-rated thoughts of who he would like to wake up next to were cut short as he started getting ready for work. From a supermodel having asked him back to her flat (as if) to realising he barely had enough milk for his cereal. Dreams and reality. Fantasy and life.

When I'm a millionaire I'll have a butler, maid, valet and a 24-hour chef, he thought to himself as he got dressed. A TV in every room, a personal cinema, a library, an arcade, a garage full of sports cars and a swimming pool. And the pool with a slide that goes from the top floor.

"Very sorry, but do you mind staying later at work tonight? Shortage of staff" blah blah. Ashley barely finished reading the message from his supervisor as he started to leave the house. Going to be a long day. He wished he owned the company. Then he'd could set the rules. No meetings before 10 or after 5, a proper canteen and a drinks machine on every floor. That was for starters.

Understandably, Ashley wasn't in a great mood when he got to the railway station, and less so when he realised the train was going to be late. Oh yes, this is the life. Even more of his life wasted as he waited for the regular experience of feeling like a squashed sardine within a herd of hippos. How awesome would it be to drive to work in a Ferrari? He'd make it a purple one. Top down, sun out, sunglasses on.

The rain that started after he got off the train was a reminder that Monday mornings sure tended to be unpleasant. Almost in life's contract. Ashley headed to his desk which was facing the window but showed nothing more glamorous than a brick wall of the building in front. Imagine looking out and being able to see a beach or Niagara Falls or the Eiffel Tower or the Taj Mahal. The Egyptian pyramids would be cool. Too much sand though.

Starting to look through his emails, Ashley then got on with his work. It wasn't exciting and it wasn't well paid but, hey, it pays the bills and his colleagues were nice enough. He wondered who he would choose to work next to? Anyone in the world. That got him thinking. Someone funny. Steve Martin would be hilarious. All those wacky faces and goofiness. Or Chris Rock. His anecdotes about growing up and his takes on dating and race would always make him hilarious. Michael MacIntyre would so be able to nail the humour in domestic life. Ashley would just have to redesign the office to make space for all three. And just keep hiring his favourite comedians.

Rating his jobs from best to worst was something Ashley did every once in a while. He definitely knew his worst one. Dressing up as a rhino outside of a "No extra charge" printer company for a very long summer. For those six weeks it was either monsoon style rain or heat like hell. Either way it really was hell. The smell. The rude customers. The boredom. The terrible money. The irate boss.

Quiet. That would be wonderful. Instead, it was all background chatter, phones ringing, traffic sounds and the odd ambulance siren. Ashley wondered if that person had survived. Sad if they didn't. Of course, it could be a police siren. He'd never known the difference. And he certainly never knew what made people want to be police officers. So much hassle. And dangerous. Pay probably wasn't great either. Must be fun to drive at fast speeds though. He would love to be a stunt car driver. How do they ever get into that? Would be definitely worth all those speeding tickets as he practised. Maybe he could do a crash course! Ha. He was definitely going to note that one down for later.

Probably should have packed a better lunch as the day had crawled to midday, he berated himself. Cold pizza. Far from healthy and far from being in its best state. Ashley wondered what it would be like to own a restaurant. They all say there's a terrible closure rate but he wouldn't make those same mistakes. What name would he give it? Something Classy. Raphianos sound elegant. And Italian. Yeah, it would be an Italian restaurant. And if that went well then for sure a bakery. And he knew what he would call it. Bake to the Future. Every bake would be linked to a film. It would obviously be a huge success.

Only 4 and ½ days left of the week, reasoned Ashley as his lunch break ended. It seemed to get shorter the longer he worked there. How had he ended up here? asked Ashley. It wasn't the first time he had wondered that. If Snakes and Ladders were more than a game it was like he had gone through the whole board missing both the ladders and the snakes and was still stuck halfway up the board. The job was ok but it wasn't what he wanted. If 28-year-old Ashley would be chatting to his 14- year-old self, he wondered what he would he have said. To be fair, education wouldn't have been the first thing that came up.

Not only was Frank, the colleague sitting nearest to him annoying, Ashley wasn't sure he was a pleasant person, either. Unlike others, Ashley wasn't bothered if Frank finished the milk or left the coffee pot empty. Or even if he didn't hold the elevator open or share his snacks. What bothered Ashley was the way Frank always took advantage of other people's nature. Whatever charity drive was used, Frank always made it seem as though he was doing everyone the favour. Even stuff like signing a card for a sick or bereaved colleague. He'd even criticise the choice of birthday cake whatever flavour. He took pleasure in the failure of others. He could never see the good in people. Ashley wondered what had made Frank so selfish and mean. What makes us what we are?

Minutes sure do crawl by. Watching the clock is a bad idea. Especially when you have to stay later for a meeting. And boy, was it dull. It would have needed a circus to liven it up.

Leaving the office was always a great feeling. One of Ashley's favourite parts of the day, especially if he'd stayed late. On his way to the station he realised he would have to go back to get his keys. Always so absentminded. He wondered if missing the train would result in some sliding doors moment. There would be no way of knowing that, mind. It would be fascinating to think what moments there had been in his life and what impact there had been.

Keeping to a set time! It shouldn't be that difficult but the train was late again. The idea for Harry Potter came after JK Rowling was on a train. Maybe if I thought more, I could come up with an idea, Ashley considered. He wondered what genre he'd write. They say write about what you know, but he'd rather do a science-fiction novel of some kind. Maybe not even set on Earth. Or even in the present.

Jackpot winnings came to mind as Ashley saw someone on the train with a scratch card. Well more than one. And they were unsuccessful with all four, the quiet swearing getting worse and slightly louder after each loss. People up and down the country would be having the same reaction most likely. He wondered if they knew how they'd spend it if they won. Ashley knew he'd totally buy that house he was thinking of earlier that day. And create a new chocolate bar.

Ignoring the urge to binge on snacks was always difficult for Ashley. The walk back from the train station was a junk food heaven. There was a pizza place, two burger diners, a chicken restaurant and a fish and chips takeaway. Not forgetting a newsagent that had all his favourite flavours of crisps, chocolate and sweets. Keeping in shape had always proved tricky. How amazing would it be if for a year he could eat whatever he wanted without suffering the consequences? He caught an unflattering reflection of himself in a shop window and frowned.

Heroic moments don't come along too often. But on the way home from the station, he found himself wondering if he had any bravery inside him. And if you only do something so as not to have to tell yourself that you are a coward, does that make you more of one, or less? There was a lot of smoke coming out of one of the buildings and the fire was pretty strong. If someone had been screaming, could he have braved the inferno to rescue someone? The question was academic as the fire fighters were already on the scene. He was glad he hadn't needed to make a decision, but he liked to think he would have made the right one.

Getting his keys through the door when getting in usually followed a playful ritual. It was all to do with a horror film he had seen as a kid. He wondered if running at the door at pace, he could hurriedly put the keys into the lock and turn it at speed first time. Nine times out of 10 he messed it up. At least half the time he'd drop his keys too.

Feet through the door, his initial thought was whether he was the first one in. If yes, time to put his feet up and catch something on TV. He tended to avoid the news. There was always some horrible story. And Ashley's reaction was always one of sadness, despair or frustration. Or occasionally fear if there was a violent psycho on the run. He could see why there was no Good News Channel. You always had to be aware of what was going on the world. And a lot of the time that wasn't pleasant.

Each of us has their own cross to bear, his father had told him all the time growing up. It was simple advice that seemed to cover a lot. Something he thought about when someone was acting out of character. His flatmate was going through a bad-break up and didn't want to talk about it.

Dinner was the one meal of the day he enjoyed. And had time to enjoy. He wondered what it would be like to work in a kitchen. He'd often watch TV when eating. Usually sports. He wasn't sure which sport he'd choose to be the world's best at. Scoring the winner in the World Cup final. Hitting the final run to win the World Series. Batting, bowling and fielding in a Man of the Series masterclass to win The Ashes. Or individual sports. Holding aloft the F1 World Championship. Winning Wimbledon and the other slams. Becoming the fastest man on Earth when setting the quickest ever time to win Olympic gold. Knocking down the favourite to capture the heavyweight title and become Mr Bad Ass.

Chatting with flatmates was usually a pleasure. There had been some quirky, some distant, some distractingly attractive ones. He counted he had lived with seven different ones over the years. He wondered what the chances of any of them becoming famous. Imagine if they were called in to a reality TV show and became super famous. Or married a royal. Or did something controversial like cheat on a quiz show or punch a celebrity. Truth was he never knew what happened to them after they left the flat. With most of them he always intended to write but never did keep in touch.

Being an only child, he always felt he needed to play the role of more than one person. He spoke to his parents most days and went to visit them at least once a fortnight. Maybe one day he'd be a parent himself. Who knows what type of parent he'd be?

And with a look at his watch, Ashley knew it was time for bed. He had meant to go earlier. He always did. He never knew how the day passed so fast. Just where did the time go?

Death = New Life

A man named Steve once lived on his own

His parents long passed, no brother or sister

Awkward and shy, he was often alone

His best friend left town, oh how he missed her!

His work wasn't stressful, he liked it so much

He owned a small business, delivering flowers.

With a love of gardening, and a Midas touch,

It still meant working all hours.

He liked his staff, they liked him right back

He always chose well whoever he hired,

But whether it was doubt, or lack of tact,

He could never connect in the way he desired.

His neighbours felt he needed a friend

Join clubs, find hobbies, get out more

He tried a few, but the fun was pretend

And being laughed at by people was the final straw.

He cried more than once and was sad for a while

He'd tried to fit in, but he'd failed again

Being outgoing wasn't his style

And it was just too big a strain.

On the anniversary of his mother's death he was at her grave

Apologising for who he was, figuring he'd let her down

When he realised it's being who you are that's brave

And making a difference in this, his town.

He went round the cemetery to note those neglected

Marking the date they had passed away

He would not guess if they were happy or tormented

Only that it'd be marked in the right way.

At the end of each day, he would go from his shop

And make a quick stop before heading home

He'd go to the cemetery, with the list and drop

The flowers on the chosen gravestone.

He told no one at work, how could he explain

That since starting it, he'd found inner peace

"No act of kindness was ever wasted", was his dad's refrain

And he felt his unhappiness start to cease.

After a few weeks things were going well,

He hadn't considered how long to do it for

He still wasn't coming out of his shell

But he found himself smiling more.

But things weren't to last, it changed one day

When laying a flower he heard a polite voice

"I didn't realise you knew my cousin. I just came to pray.

But no need to explain, that's your choice."

She had the kindest eyes he'd ever seen

His felt his heart melt and skip a beat

This felt to him like a Hollywood movie scene

And yet what an odd place to meet.

He stared at her as wondering how honest he should be
He could lie and she'd never know
But his mum told him the truth sets you free
And they were words he promised to follow.

So he explained about being a misfit
But wanting those forgotten remembered on their birthday
Which sounded a bit strange he had to admit
But he wanted to make a difference, even in a small way.

The woman was rather surprised and in a little shock
It seemed so odd a stranger could be so kind
She felt others might be guarded, or feel the need to mock
But honesty and kindness can be hard to find.

She was intrigued and wanted to know more
Were his motives pure, did he really have a good heart?
She needed to be cautious as she'd been tricked before
So suggesting a coffee was a good start.

They were both odd souls but had really connected

Talking weeks on end, losing track of time

Now they were a couple, she reflected

Why not become of the same mind?

She reasoned that joining forces they could do more together

Do something grander, not just small scale

Something that wouldn't fade but last forever

With an idea that she felt couldn't fail.

The bookstore she ran hosted a fundraiser night

To raise money to make all headstones pristine

The whole community became involved, quite the sight

Some not just giving money, but offering to clean.

So much was raised, it became a big local story

People were intrigued and inspired by what they had done

Two lost souls finding each other and then wider glory

A reminder that each of us can still be ourselves and find someone.

Questions, Answers, Questions

As a child, while playing indoors with your football, you accidentally break your mother's prize vase. It was a precious and long-held family heirloom. Knowing she will be back from shopping soon and the discovery is only a short time away, you decide to:

A)   Admit everything to your mother. Knowing full well how mad she will be, you offer to get a job helping to deliver local newspapers so you can buy her a gift as an apology

B)   Initially think about pretending it wasn't you, but hope if you cry as you say sorry she won't be as mad ✔

C)   Deny all knowledge as your mother cannot prove it was you, even though you see your mother's face sadden as she knows you are lying

D)   Blame it on the cleaner who your mother then fires

You hear that the answers for a really important quiz are available from the school's most cunning and entrepreneurial bad boy. What happens?

A)   Nothing. That whole cheating thing is repulsive to you. Besides you've revised for it ✔

B)   After some thought, nothing. You're tempted, but you just can't risk getting caught

C)   You go for it. Doing well will buy you a lot of brownie points

D)   You are the student selling the papers

It's high school and the big prom is coming up. You hear rumours that an overweight, unattractive girl is under the impression that you fancy her and will ask her to the dance. You:

A)   Immediately and discretely let her one of her friends know that you aren't the slightest bit interested

B)   Allow the rumour to go on a little longer while you bask in the glory of a raised profile before you decide to tell her you never fancied her

C)   Decide to let it go as long as it can. It looks like being quite the anecdote ✔

D)   Pretend to fancy her back and take pleasure in seeing her get all excited before you crush her spirit at the last minute and admit it was all a joke

A beautiful new girl joins your college. You and your long-time best friend fancy her and each of you think they have a good chance. In order to keep the peace, you both decide to make a pact to avoid pursuing her. Do you keep to it?

A)   For sure. You've been through a lot and no girl is worth destroying the friendship for

B)   You ask her out behind your friend's back but feel too guilty to properly go through with anything and never tell your friend anything

C)   After thinking it over, you decide that you want to scrap the pact. Whoever wins, wins.

D)   You ignore the pact. You sabotage your best friend's chances through a mixture of exaggerated truths and sneaky lies and successfully make a big play to win her over ✔

You've been working your way up the ladder at the big office you work in. Things are going well, if a little slow. One day, your boss accidentally includes you in an email that would cause him huge grief if you decide to share it with his superiors. He begs you not to do anything. What's your response?

A)   It's disappointing. He's always been a solid boss and you thought he was a better man than that. While making it clear you don't approve, you confirm with him that you won't be forwarding it to anyone else

B)   There's an upcoming conference work trip being held in Hawaii that you thought you deserved to be included in. You make it clear he has your permanent discretion, but remind him that there's still space for the Hawaii conference, which he happily agrees to ✔

C)   You have him by the balls and you're prepared to play hardball. A pay rise, a promotion and a new office or you're taking him down

D)   You make a list of outrageous demands that you know he can't match. You aren't swayed by his desperate pleas for clemency and you let his superiors know

Your next-door neighbour, who has always gone out of his way to be helpful to you, is falling apart as his marriage is collapsing. Seeing him in such obvious discomfort and in his time of need:

A)   You spend more time with him. You make a big effort to keep him busy, keep his spirits high and be a shoulder for him to lean on

B)   You don't want to spend any time with him, but you do make sure to ask how he is doing and be careful with what you say

C) You don't really notice him too much as your attention is on the hot new blonde who has moved in a few doors down ✔

D) You've always thought his wife was hot. Good time to be making a move

A highly unpleasant, but rather wealthy, relative has long been disinherited by the rest of the family for his cruel and offensive treatment of others. Through a friend who has connections to a nearby hospice, you realise that while he hasn't changed his nature, he is keen to leave his money to an heir. What's your next move?

A) The guy was a disgrace to the family in every way possible. You want nothing to do with him or his money ✔

B) You're tempted. You visit him, but no. You can't even pretend to like him

C) It's only a few visits within a two to three-week period. You also decide to leave a small amount to the nurses and hospice

D) You were owed a break. You use any manner of charm and deception to ensure you get every last penny

You finally find the perfect woman and you're crazy about her. Things are going perfectly and when you propose she immediately accepts. At an airport bar on a work trip you spot a former popstar. You used to have her on your wall, she still looks great and is clearly interested in taking things further that night. What do you do?

A) You politely tell her that while you're incredibly flattered, you are very much taken. You head back to your hotel room alone

B) You don't, but there is the odd time over the years when you find yourself wondering if you should have ✔

C) You sure do. A celebrity doesn't count the same and you owe it to your younger self

D) You sleep with her and sell your story. Though she's no longer active, she's still well-known and you can get a nice payday

The weekend football team your son plays for have been fighting for the championship all season. Your wife has been the Soccer Mum as part of a league car pool. In the crucial final game, your son begs you to attend as moral support. Your response?

A) Of course, you'll go! You've been following the team's fortunes all season. You've been giving him extra training and haven't missed a game ✔

B) You've been to quite a few of them anyway, even though the games have been annoyingly early and the coach is a nightmare

C) You go out the night before for a colleague's drinks. After oversleeping, you turn up hungover and dishevelled but catch most of the second half

D) You've already got something booked. You could rearrange but it would be a hassle. Your father never attended any of your sporting stuff and you got over it

After feeling unwell you visit your doctor. She does some tests and it's not good news. You only have a few months to live. Further tests and diagnosis only confirm it. How do you look back on your life?

A) There are plenty of people worse off and far too many who died young. You've had a good innings. Being informed in this manner means you can properly say goodbye to everyone

B) You are in shock for several days. After some good advice, you make a list of things to do and set about completing them and thinking back on the good times you've had ✔

C) The sadness and bitterness last a few weeks but you are able to shake it off and enjoy the rest of your life unleashed. And now there's no need to worry about the effects of drinking, smoking, etc

D) It's not fair you getting such bad news. Just that same day there was an article about a multiple murderer who lived to over 100. You won't have enough time to achieve all you wanted to and you burn a lot of the bridges you made throughout your life

Have you passed? Is there anything you wish you could answer differently?

Background Notes

Within Twilight

The inspiration came from a dream. The idea of a guy asking a strange and magical figure for a wish. That wish ended with a rope dissolving across the ocean and drowning. That premise of making all the wishes have disastrous results felt too limiting and there was more imagination with mixing things up.

After Life

The first one written for this collection and was always intended to be the opening story. It marked a real change in my writing style. Reflects my love of art and card games.

Breaking Through the Fourth Page

The title is drawn from characters who break the fourth wall in TV. It was written a few years ago, but I rewrote it, adding more humour and trivia.

Punbelievable

I have always had fun with puns. The title came very easily, and this story was definitely the most fun to write. The idea initially involved three friends, but it became obvious very early on that it would be smoother dialogue between two friends, and the waiter could then be more involved.

Just Imagining Today

Originally called Z-A & A-Z. I wrote several features of 'A Life Within a Day' throughout my years of education, so writing one with a different creative angle was both fun and challenging.

Death = New Life

The idea of a lonely man finding love at a cemetery was one that I'd had for a while and came before the concept of having the story within a poem.

Questions, Answers, Questions

The big question with this was whether to include the ticks. But as well as giving its own story, it also meant there was more resonance in the final line.

Printed in Dunstable, United Kingdom